BROWN LIKE ME

by Noelle Lamperti
with her
Friends and Family

New Victoria Publishers
Norwich, Vermont

Published by New Victoria Publishers Inc., PO Box 27, Norwich, VT 05055
A Feminist Literary and Cultural organization founded in 1976.

Drawings by Noelle Lamperti and the children of the Learning School
Photos by Matthew Lamperti and Beth Dingman
Printed in Hong Kong
New edition
2 3 4 5 2002
Originally published under the title: Noelle's Brown Book, New Victoria, 1976

Library of Congress Cataloging-in-Publication Data

Lamperti, Noelle.
Brown like me / by Noelle Lamperti and friends. -- New ed.
p. cm.
Rev. ed. of : Noelle's brown book.
Summary: A little girl named Noelle tells how she likes to go looking for things that are brown like her.
ISBN 1-892281-03-1
1. Afro-Americans--Juvenile fiction. 2. Children's writings, American. [1. Afro-Americans--Fiction. 2. Brown--Fiction. 3. Children's writings.] I. Noelle's brown book. II. Title.
PZ7.L18445Bo 1999
[E] --dc21 98-51132
CIP
AC

When the publishers asked me to write something about *Noelle's Brown Book*, I pulled out our family's well-worn copy of the original book. I read it often to my son and later, to my daughter who, like Noelle, is brown and adopted. Growing up in a white family, she too was sometimes "lonesome for brown."

As a parent and as a mental health professional, I recommend this book to parents and children of all colors. In celebrating families and the color brown, this book enriches all of us and is sure to delight a whole new generation of "strong brown" children.

Jacqueline Wallen, PhD, MSW
Associate Professor
Department of Family Studies
University of Maryland, College Park

Hi,
I'm Noelle,
a girl
who likes
brown.

I like to
look
for things
that are
brown
like me.

Here I am with my family at the lake.
My brother, Matt is taking the picture.

My friend
Rosie has
brown eyes
and brown
skin like me.

Sometimes Rosie
likes to look for
brown with me.

Rosie finds some cool brown boots.

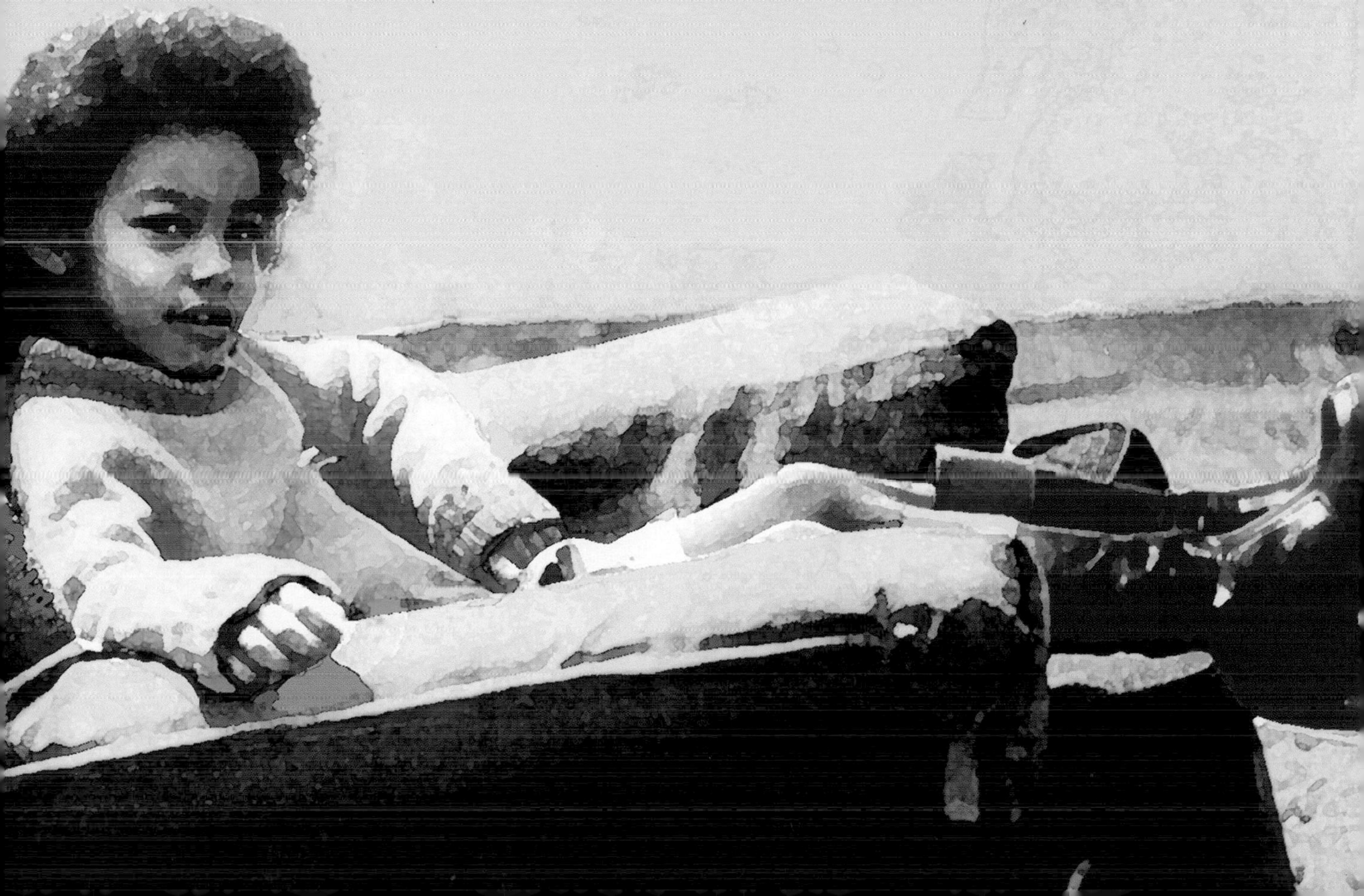

My friend
Holly and I
like to bake
brownies.

They are
yummy brown
chocolate.

Judy and I look for brown on her shaggy brown horse.

We find two
friendly brown goats.

My dog Taco has brown spots.

Amelia holds
me up high
to pick
some sweet,
brown pears.

Here I am in a pile
of brown leaves.

This is my brown house.

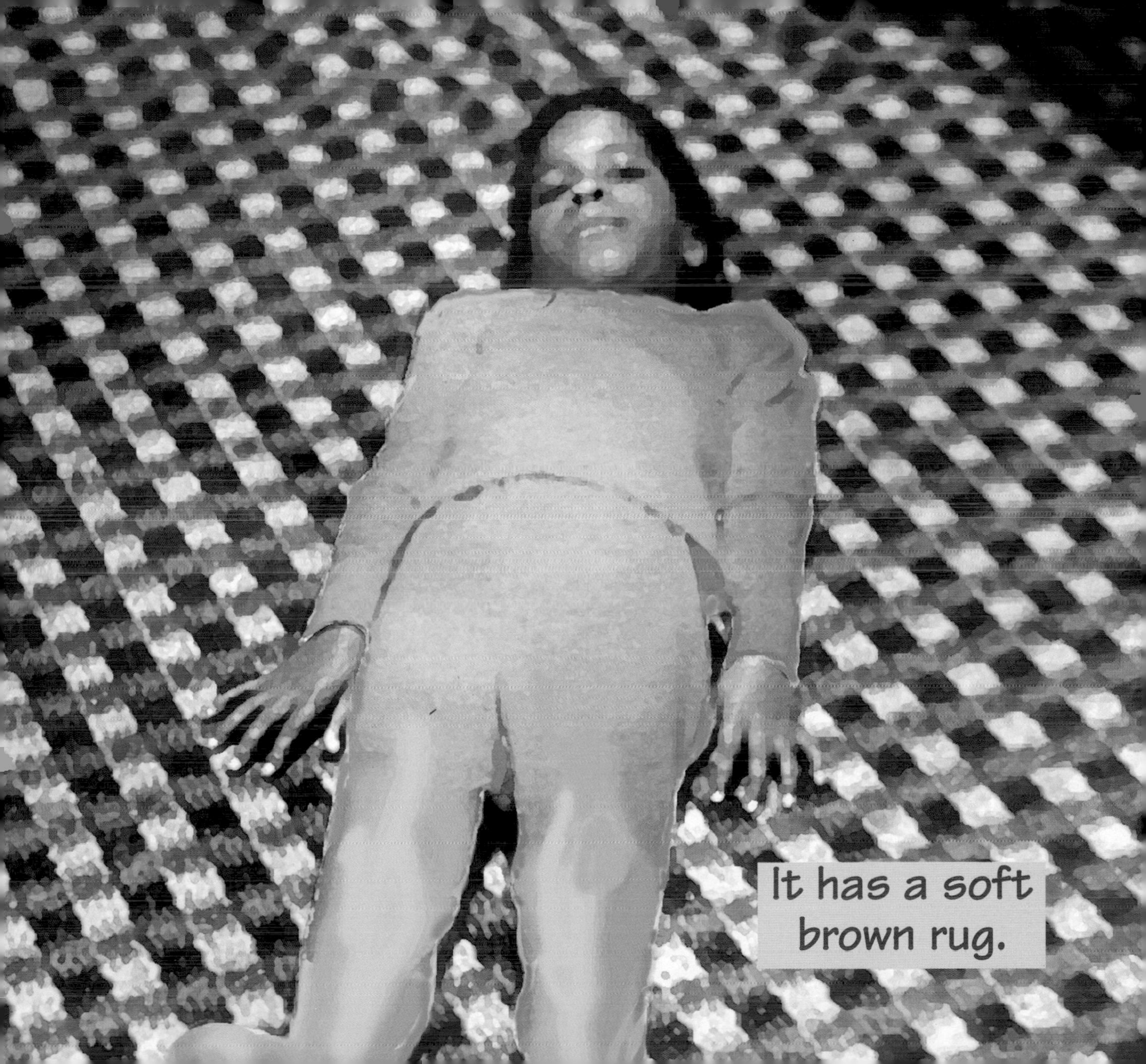

It has a soft
brown rug.

My mom helps
me find brown.
She has
brown crinkly
hair like mine.

I like to put on
my shiny new
brown boots
and brown
leather jacket.

And get on
my brother
Matt's
big brown
motorcycle.

We go looking for brown together. His motorcycle is nice and loud.

We ride on the
motorcycle to
the beach to
find brown sand.

Sometimes
I go looking
for brown
by myself.

I find
some fuzzy
brown bees.

Here is a
picture I
drew
of the
brown bees
and their
brown hive.

Come with me.
Let's look
for brown
together.

brown suger bowl

violin

brown bear

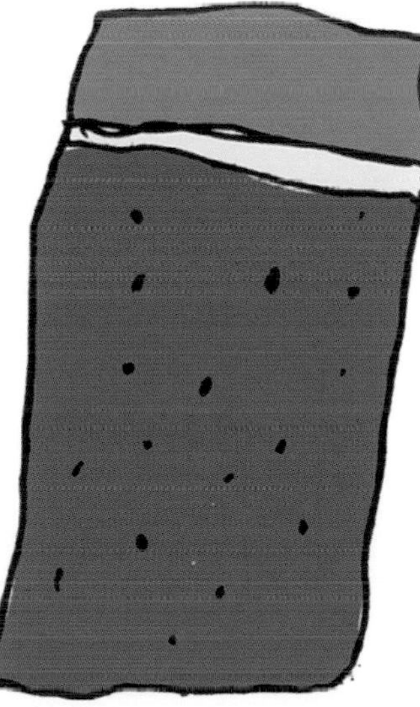

brown peanut butter

Can you
find
more
brown?
FIRE FIGHTER

When I am
lonesome for brown
I look in the mirror.

I can see my
bright brown eyes,
curly brown hair,
and smooth
brown skin.

I am strong brown.

I was reminded of the importance of this book when ten years after it was published I went into the local library in Hanover, New Hampshire. A small brown girl about six years old saw me and I overheard her saying to her adoptive mother, "Mom, is that Noelle?"

Her mother looked at me and I heard her say, "I'm not sure; why don't we ask." They stopped me and the woman asked if I was Noelle from the *Brown Book*. I told her that I was and she said that the book had been very important to them and that they read it all the time.

Helping to create the *Brown Book* was a wonderful experience for me. Being encouraged to create both a storyline and drawings made me feel special. Most importantly, writing this book was an affirmation of who I was and am. In a community where very few people looked like me, the *Brown Book* was something that I could look to and be reminded that being brown and looking different was a good thing.

I think that this book is great for everyone in its celebration of diversity.

Noelle

Photo by John Lamperti